GIRLS SURVIVE

Girls Survive is published by Stone Arch Books, an imprint of Capstone.
1710 Roe Crest Drive
North Mankato, Minnesota 56003
www.capstonepub.com

Library of Congress Cataloging-in-Publication Data is available on the Library of Congress website.

ISBN: 978-1-4965-9692-5 (hardcover)
ISBN: 978-1-4965-9912-4 (paperback)
ISBN: 978-1-4965-9763-2 (eBook PDF)

Summary: In 1980s Washington state, Mount St. Helens is rumbling. Twelve-year-old Maribel isn't concerned at first, despite officials evacuating her neighborhood. Her family is convinced it's just a precaution, even as the mountain continues to rumble. Maribel decides to disobey orders and return home for items she and her sister left behind—just as the volcano finally erupts. As ash rains down, Maribel realizes she must learn to focus if she's going to survive.

Image Credits
Shutterstock: Aaron Rutten, 106, RedKoala, design element, Spalnic, (watercolor) design element

Designer: Kayla Rossow

MARIBEL

VERSUS THE VOLCANO

A Mount St. Helens Survival Story

by Sarah Hannah Gómez

illustrated by Jane Pica

STONE ARCH BOOKS
a capstone imprint

CHAPTER ONE

"Thanks a lot, Maribel! Because of you, I have to wait until tomorrow to pick up my pictures!" my sister, Lupe, snapped as we walked down the hallway at school. "Why did you have to get in trouble *again*?"

I looked at my watch. "It's only three-forty. That's plenty of time to make it to the photo store."

Lupe shook her head. "We missed the bus because *you* had to stay after class," she said. "Now we have to call Mom and wait for her to pick us up. By the time we get there, the store will be closed."

I sighed. It wasn't like I had stayed after class on purpose. But after the fourth time my teacher, Mr. Jennings, had called on me in social studies with no response—"Miss Reyes, are you listening?"—he'd gotten mad.

He'd told me to come to his classroom after school so we could talk about "my continued failure to stay focused on course content." That basically meant I had a bad habit of daydreaming during class.

As my older sister, Lupe always waited for me so we could catch the bus together after school. Seventh and eighth grades had different lunch periods, though, so I hadn't been able to warn her that I would be out late.

So now I was in trouble with my social studies teacher *and* my sister. And when we got home and Lupe told my parents why we had missed the bus, I would be in trouble with them too.

I didn't daydream in class on purpose. It was just that a teacher would say something, and that would make me think of something I had seen on television or read in a book. That would remind me of something that had happened at lunch the day before and . . . before I knew it, everyone in class was looking at me because I had no idea what was going on.

I wasn't *trying* to be disrespectful to my teachers. It just sort of happened.

"Well," I said, "it's only Thursday. You'll be able to go pick up your pictures tomorrow."

Lupe glared at me. "I wanted my photos *today.* I was going to show them to Ms. Ybarra tomorrow."

"I'll make it up to you," I promised.

I didn't know how I would do that, but I really was sorry. Lupe loved photography. She went to the photo store nearly every week to have film developed. My parents even joked about building her a darkroom so she could develop photos herself. But our nana, who had lived with us since I was a baby, put her foot down. She said that if we wanted to have that many chemicals in the house, she would move out.

I was pretty sure she was exaggerating, but it was enough to make Mami and Dad change their minds.

Lupe and I were still bickering when we reached my locker. I spun the dial on the combination lock silently while my sister chewed me out.

"OK," I said, stashing my books. "Let's go."

I slammed my locker door, and suddenly I was on my back on the floor.

I couldn't get up. The floor was moving beneath me. The row of lockers above me rattled. I tried to look for my sister, but my eyes wouldn't focus.

And then, just like that, everything was still—*too* still. It was like the world had gone from off the rails to moving backward in slow motion.

Once my gaze settled, I could see Lupe. She was on the floor, braced against the lockers. Her mouth was wide open, and the color had drained from her face.

I looked past her. At the end of the empty hallway, just before the double doors, the narrow glass case that held school trophies for sports and other events was wobbling dramatically. As I watched, it stopped its wobbling and tipped over.

Crash! It fell to the ground. The glass shattered.

I jolted. I felt as unsteady as the trophy case.

"What was that?" Lupe whispered. She tried to gulp in some air, but I heard a wheeze.

Lupe didn't like to draw attention to it—or herself—but she had asthma. When she was stressed out or angry—like she'd been with me today—her lungs acted up.

"You felt it too?" I asked. It was almost a relief to know I hadn't just slammed the locker shut with too much force and knocked myself over.

"Of course I felt it." Lupe wheezed again.

She pushed herself up to standing, then held her hand out and helped me to my feet. I still felt shaky, even though the world around me had stopped moving.

Just then a classroom door opened behind us. "What was that?" a voice gasped.

I turned and saw Ms. Ybarra, the art teacher—and Lupe's favorite person in the whole world, it seemed. When she saw us, Ms. Ybarra's eyes widened in concern.

"Oh, girls, are you OK?" She rushed over to check on us.

"We're OK," Lupe said.

"What was that?" I asked. "An earthquake?"

Ms. Ybarra nodded. "A big one, I think. I'm glad you two weren't standing near anything heavy."

Lupe pointed to the shattered trophy case. "Luckily we missed that," she said.

Ms. Ybarra walked over to inspect the mess. "I'll have to call the custodian to clean it up so nobody steps on any of the glass," she said. She turned back to us. "What are you two still doing here? There aren't any after-school activities today."

"We missed the bus," I said. Lupe poked me in the side. "Well, *I* missed the bus. And Lupe waited for me, so she missed it too. We were going to call our mom for a ride." I looked at my sister. "Or maybe we can just walk home. It's only about three miles."

Ms. Ybarra shook her head. "Oh, no, no, no. Not after an earthquake like that. I'll drive you girls. I would never forgive myself if something happened while you two were on your own. Your parents wouldn't forgive me, either. Come with me."

Lupe and I followed Ms. Ybarra to the office to radio the custodian, then to the teachers' parking lot.

She had given Lupe rides home after art club, but I had never been in her car before.

A teacher's car! I thought as we approached the little red hatchback. It seemed forbidden and almost unnatural, as if I shouldn't know that teachers had lives outside of school.

As we turned out of the school parking lot, Ms. Ybarra rapped her knuckles on the car window. She gestured to the gigantic mountain peak—the major landmark in Cougar, Washington, where we lived—visible against the blue sky.

"Take a look at Lawetlat'la," she said with a nod. "I think we've found the culprit behind our earthquake."

I craned my neck to see. "What's that?" I asked. "All I see is Mount St. Helens."

"*Lawetlat'la* is the mountain's real name," Ms. Ybarra said. "It's the name the Cowlitz people gave it long before Europeans came here and renamed it Mount St. Helens. I'm surprised you haven't learned that from Mr. Jennings."

I was too. Then again, maybe I'd just missed it—although I didn't want to tell Ms. Ybarra that. I was already in enough trouble for daydreaming.

"You students should know all of Washington history, not just the American part," Ms. Ybarra continued. "You have classmates who are Cowlitz. They may not have a reservation, but this is still their ancestral land."

"Lawetlat'la," Lupe said slowly. "Is that why one of the hiking trails is called Loowit? And Loowit Falls? Are they related?"

"Yes!" Ms. Ybarra said. "And if memory serves me, I believe the word *Lawetlat'la* means 'the Smoker.' Seems appropriate, huh?" She gestured to the mountain again.

I stared out the window—Ms. Ybarra was right. The mountain wasn't just a mountain. Everyone

knew it had been a volcano in the past, but I had
never seen it like this. Heavy clouds of smoke were
pouring out of it like steam from a teakettle.

I thought of my nana's teakettle at home and
how it would shriek and sing when the water
came to a boil. If I were close to the summit of
the mountain, would I hear it make noise, or was
it silent? When volcanoes erupted, did they fill the
summit like a mug of tea with a tea bag, or did
they pour out and spill over everything?

CHAPTER TWO

"Hey, Maribel! Catch!" Before I could react, a Frisbee whizzed past me. It bounced on the grass of the picnic area where my family and I, along with many others, were spending the day.

I looked up to see who had thrown the disc. It wasn't Lupe. She was sitting on the grass right next to me, fiddling with her camera.

But I saw Marcus Johnson, the son of one of my mom's coworkers, coming from the parking lot and waving at me. Our parents were good friends, and we had invited the Johnsons out to the mountain for

a picnic at one of the lookout points. Marcus was also in my grade at school, but we didn't have any classes together.

"Hi, Marcus!" I said.

I went to retrieve the Frisbee, gripped it close to my chest, and then sent it spiraling back to him. But the person who caught it wasn't Marcus—it was his dad, who quickly sent it back. I had to leap to catch it.

I held off on returning it right away. Marcus's mother was behind them. She was holding a picnic basket in one hand and a tote bag bursting with blankets in the other.

"Hi, Mr. and Mrs. Johnson!" I said.

I hurried over and took Mrs. Johnson's picnic basket, setting it down next to my family's. We had staked out a good spot at the lookout point. It was one of our favorite places for picnics—only twenty minutes away from home—but it was our first time being there since the earthquake.

There had been countless tiny earthquakes since then. I had almost come to expect them. I felt like I was constantly waiting to trip over nothing or to see pictures askew on the wall—there was something quirky to expect every day.

Many of my classmates had been out to see "the Smoker" up close in the past couple weeks. Lupe and I had begged our parents until they finally agreed to a picnic.

Now that we were here, it was unlike anything I had ever seen before. The mountain had grown in size and changed shape over the past few weeks, developing a bulge on its side. It was almost as if it was growing another mountain inside it.

Who needs a classroom science experiment when you can watch a life-size mountain burp steam and ash into the air? I thought.

Lots of other people clearly had the same idea. The lookout point was crowded today. There were babies in strollers, scientists taking measurements and photographs, hikers consulting maps, and families picnicking on blankets.

"We're living history!" Dad had told us when we first arrived.

After the Johnsons had set up their picnic, Marcus asked me to throw him the Frisbee.

"Go over there, away from all the people," said Mrs. Johnson. She pointed to a patch of land in the shadow of a line of trees. "See if any of the other kids want to join you!"

Marcus was already rounding up some of the classmates of ours he had found. I went over to my sister and tugged her arm.

"Come on, Lupe," I said. "Put down your camera and play Frisbee with us."

Lupe sighed and carefully put the lens cap on the camera. "Nana," she said to our grandmother, "will you make sure nothing happens to my camera?"

"Of course, *m'ija*," Nana said, looking up from dipping a chip into a container of salsa. She held her hand out, and Lupe handed over the camera. "Don't forget to take your inhaler," Nana added.

Lupe blushed and ducked her head, but she obediently reached into the camera bag she had brought with her. A moment later, she pulled out her asthma inhaler. Glancing around to make sure no one was watching, she took a big puff of air in. Then she hurriedly stuffed the inhaler back into the bag.

I shook my head. My sister was so ashamed of her inhaler. It was as if she thought it made her weak or uncool to have asthma. She was always trying to sneak her inhaler out of her schoolbag and leave it at home whenever we went somewhere. It didn't make sense to me.

Why be embarrassed of something you can't control? I always thought.

Lupe, Marcus, and I played Frisbee with other neighborhood kids until our parents called us to eat lunch. Everything was calm for awhile. But then, when we were eating the cookies Mrs. Johnson had baked for dessert, a massive *boom!* shook the air.

My head jerked straight up. Everybody at the lookout point seemed to jump about a mile. It sounded like the loudest jet engine of all time. I felt the earth shake beneath my feet, just like it had at school a month ago. The vibration went all the way up my body.

High above us, Mount St. Helens had puffed out a particularly large cloud of steam. I could see ash slowly raining down. It reminded me of how fireworks looked as they died out and dropped from the sky.

"OK, kids!" my dad called. "We're going to pack it in. Looks like Mount St. Helens is not happy we all decided to visit today."

I sighed and turned to Marcus and the other kids we'd been playing with. "See you at school," I said.

"Bye," Marcus replied sadly. "See you later, Mr. and Mrs. Reyes," he called to my parents.

So much for a fun Sunday, I thought as Lupe and I helped our parents and grandma carry our things to the car.

We headed home, but things didn't get any calmer as we drove to our house. On nearly every block, it seemed, there were police cruisers and park ranger cars. People in uniforms were walking up and down the sidewalks and standing on porches.

"What's going on?" I asked as I looked out the window.

Mami didn't slow the car down, but Dad answered. "I don't know. You'd almost think we were in some kind of cop show."

"I don't like the look of this," Nana said.

"Me neither," Mami agreed.

Thankfully there were no cars on our street when we arrived home, so we unpacked our picnic things and went inside. Lupe and I headed upstairs to finish our homework. I hadn't done more than a few questions on my practice math quiz when I heard the doorbell ring.

Nana must have opened the door, because I heard her calling for my father in Spanish, asking him to come to the door and translate. Nana spoke English almost perfectly, but sometimes she liked to pretend otherwise—usually when she didn't like what she was hearing or the person talking.

From upstairs I heard my parents both make their way to the front door. All of a sudden, I had a bad feeling in my chest. When I looked up from my homework and across the hallway at my sister's bedroom, she was looking straight back at me. I knew we were thinking the same thing:

Something is wrong.

Lupe and I slid out of our chairs and quietly crept toward the stairs. From there we had a view of the door but couldn't see who stood outside it.

"That's ridiculous," Dad was saying. "We were just there. Not safe to be right there at the base of the mountain, sure. But an eruption?"

"There's no way," Mami added.

Lupe nodded to me, and we walked downstairs. I was no longer worried about interrupting. I needed to know what was going on.

Nana saw us and motioned for Lupe and me to join the adults at the door. Dad and Mami were talking to a police officer. When he saw us approach, the officer nodded his head at us.

"Good evening, young ladies," he said. "I'm sorry to bother you like this. I'm sure you're just getting ready for bed."

"Bed?" I said. "We're not babies. It's only six. We haven't even had dinner yet!"

Mami shook her head at me, as if to say,
Not now, Maribel.

"I'm afraid dinner is going to have to be
at a friend's or out at a restaurant tonight," the
policeman said.

"What are you talking about?" Lupe demanded.
"We never go out to eat on a school night."

Dad sighed and held up his hand. "Apparently
tonight we will."

"Why?" I asked, still confused.

"Because," said the police officer, "you're being
evacuated."

CHAPTER THREE

Cougar, Washington
April 30, 1980
6:02 p.m.

"Evacuated? What do you mean, 'evacuated'?"

Mami turned to look at us. "Apparently we live in what they're calling the red zone," she explained. "The police are evacuating everyone who lives within twelve miles of the volcano. That includes us here in Cougar. They think it's going to erupt."

"When?" Lupe asked.

"Any minute now, this man says," Dad said.

The police officer cleared his throat. "Not any minute as in *tonight*," he said. "But very likely in the near future. We think. I'm not really a scientist, you know. I can't tell you a precise date. But we're doing this for your safety. You and all of your neighbors."

I couldn't believe what I was hearing. First, earthquake after earthquake. Now this.

If it it's just steam escaping from the mountain, why is everyone so worried? I wondered. *It's not like we live right at the foot of Mount St. Helens.*

It all seemed over-the-top. We had to drive at least fifteen minutes to get home, winding through the mountain roads. Nothing that spurted out of Mount St. Helens could get that far.

It was sputtering this afternoon, and it didn't even hit any of the picnickers, I thought.

Mami clearly agreed with me. "This is ridiculous," she said to the policeman. "We're miles from the mountain. I can understand evacuating people at the lodge at Spirit Lake, but what danger could we possibly be in? Who would build a town near a volcano that had any chance of actually erupting? She's just . . . letting off steam."

Nobody laughed.

"I really am sorry to do this," the officer said. "But it's a mandatory evacuation. You can take some time to pack a few bags, but then we will be escorting this block out of the neighborhood to safety. You can't stay here."

"Where are we supposed to go?" Lupe asked.

"We have a list of motels outside the red zone with vacancies," the policeman offered. "Or maybe you can call a friend or relative and stay with them?"

Dad crossed his arms and glared.

Nana threw her hands up in exasperation. "*Ándale, pues. Voy a llamar a* Roberta," she said.

"That's a good idea," Mami said, nodding at Nana's suggestion. "The Johnsons live in Yale, outside the evacuation area. I'm sure we can stay with them."

"OK, then," the police officer said. "I'll leave you to it. We're asking everyone to be outside in fifteen minutes, ready to go."

He turned to leave, then spun around on his heels to face us again. "Between you and me, I'm sure you'll be back in your house by Tuesday," he said. "The government will realize all those geologists are taking things too far, and everyone will lighten up and go home."

"Thanks, officer," Dad said. He gave the policeman a wave, then took hold of the door and pushed it closed. "Well, girls," he said, turning to us. "I guess you should go pack an overnight bag and your school things. I'll pack for myself and your mom while she helps your nana."

Nana had already left the room for the kitchen, where the phone was. I could hear her explaining the situation to Mrs. Johnson as I made my way up the stairs.

In my room, I opened my dresser and started pulling clothes out, making a small pile on my bed that I figured would last me three days. Then I carefully put my half-finished homework in my backpack along with all my textbooks, except one.

Where is my social studies book? I thought. The last thing I needed was to forget my textbook and give Mr. Jennings *another* reason to be mad at me.

I got down on my knees and peeked under my bed. *Aha!* I placed the book on my desk and tried to think of what else I would need to pack for the week.

As I did, my eyes fell on the cover of my textbook. There was a collage of images on it, but only one stood out to me now—a picture of two men, ancient Romans, in togas.

We hadn't spent too much time on ancient Rome. Mr. Jennings had said the Romans were too similar to ancient Greeks and that we had better move on to other topics. But we *had* learned about Pompeii, the town that had been completely destroyed by . . . a volcano!

I gasped.

Pompeii had been a town like any other until Mount Vesuvius had erupted, blanketing the entire place in lava. Thousands had been killed. Later, when the town was excavated, archaeologists found much of it perfectly preserved. It was as if it had been frozen in time.

I stopped in my tracks.

What if . . .

Before I could finish my thought, Mami called up the stairs: "Girls, hurry up!"

Lupe and I lugged our things downstairs and dropped them at our feet. Mami, Dad, and Nana were already waiting by the front door with their own bags.

"Now, I don't want you to worry at all, girls," Dad said. "Like the police officer said, they're doing their jobs and trying to make everyone feel safe. But we'll be home before you know it. Everyone is overreacting. Yes, Mount St. Helens is a volcano, but you saw it today—we all did. It's not going to *explode*. It'll keep letting off little bits of steam and gas, and then it'll settle right down. You'll see."

Mami nodded in agreement. "Nana spoke to Mrs. Johnson. She'll have dinner ready for all of us," she said. "It'll be fun! Like a mini vacation." It didn't seem like she believed what she was saying.

Lupe nodded and handed one of her bags to Dad, who carried it outside. Before my sister could follow him, I grabbed her arm.

"Lupe," I hissed. "Did you ever learn about Pompeii?"

"Everybody's heard of Pompeii," she said, rolling her eyes. She hoisted her other bag up and put it on her shoulder.

"Is Mount St. Helens like Vesuvius?" I asked.

Lupe shot me an annoyed look. "What? Don't be ridiculous. It's nothing like that. That's ancient history."

"But—"

Lupe huffed and marched out the door. "Come on, Maribel!" she called without looking back.

I sighed in frustration. Sometimes big sisters could be exasperating.

My parents loaded everything into the car, and we set off for the Johnsons' house. Soon everyone was guessing what we would be having for dinner and wondering who would be more surprised to see us—Marcus or his father.

I was the only one who didn't participate in the conversation. I just looked up at the mountain, still spewing, and shivered, even though I wasn't cold. It had seemed so fun that afternoon, watching it spurt out all that gas and steam. But now, all I could think about were those people in Pompeii. I wondered if they too had seen gas and steam and thought there was nothing to worry about.

CHAPTER FOUR

The Johnsons' house
Yale, Washington
May 17, 1980
6:34 p.m.

The police officer was wrong. We didn't go home by Tuesday. Almost three weeks later, we were *still* staying with the Johnsons.

Everyone was getting on each other's nerves. There was never enough hot water in the morning for eight showers. Lupe had forgotten her camera at our house, and she was more and more upset about it every day. Mami and Mrs. Johnson, who were usually good friends, were snippy with each other. And Dad and Mr. Johnson were barely speaking to each other.

I was getting really tired of having to do laundry all the time. Even though Mami had taken us shopping for a few things, it still felt like I barely had any clothes to wear before I was back at the washing machine.

Lupe had even cried about it. According to her, she was the laughingstock of the eighth grade because she was stuck wearing the same outfits every week.

But the worst part of the whole thing was Nana. She seemed more and more tired every day. She usually laughed and told stories and baked treats, but now she was quiet all the time and spent a lot of the day in bed.

The whole world seemed gloomier. We weren't the only kids at school who had been evacuated or who were hosting evacuees. Teachers seemed overly worried about the volcano some days, making us go through safety drills. Other days, they were *too* cheery, telling us tests were canceled or we had extra time at lunch.

Nothing was right. I just wanted to go home and have everything go back to normal.

Then, finally, we got some good news.

"The neighbors are fed up," Mami said at Saturday dinner. "They say if it's been this long and nothing has happened, nothing *will* happen. The authorities *still* won't let people return to their houses permanently. But they've agreed to give us a short window to run home and grab more of our stuff. But we have to go now. Girls, get your shoes."

"Yes!" I cheered.

"My camera!" cried Lupe.

"My books!" Mami cheered.

"My nice shoes," Dad said with a grin. He had been wearing his ratty old sneakers every day because he had forgotten to change his shoes when we left.

"*Mis fotos*," Nana said from the easy chair where she had been spending most of her time out of bed. She had countless old photos from her childhood in Mexico, from her wedding to my tata, from Mami's childhood.

She loved taking them out, and I loved hearing her stories over and over again. They were one of the few things that could keep my mind from spinning out of control. Focusing on those let me think about only one thing instead of five.

Nana leaned into the arms of the chair to press herself up. Too late, the seven of us looked over at her and realized what was happening. As she took a step forward, Nana lost her balance. She fell to the ground with a horrible *thud!*

"Nana!" I shouted.

Nana howled and writhed on the floor in pain. We all rushed toward her. Mami held Lupe and me back as Dad knelt by Nana's side. He tried to help her to her feet, but she moaned and could barely stand.

"I think it's her hip," he said. "We need to take her to the hospital."

Mami nodded. "Girls, stay here."

"But what about our things?" I asked.

"I was going to get my camera!" Lupe wailed.

"Don't you think this is a little more important?" Dad snapped.

"Sorry," Lupe mumbled. I looked down, ashamed.

"We'll see about going to the house tomorrow morning," Mami said.

With that, she and Dad carefully scooped up our tiny, frail nana into their arms. They carried her out of the house, leaving Lupe and me behind. Mrs. Johnson came and hugged us close to her.

They still weren't back by the time we went to bed. That wasn't a good sign. Nana must be staying overnight, and I knew Mami and Dad wouldn't leave her by herself.

I needed a distraction from worrying about Nana, and Lupe was still upset over her camera, so I started brainstorming. Mami and Dad were taking care of Nana, and I didn't want to ask the Johnsons to drive us to our house.

It's ridiculous, I thought. *We don't even live that far away.*

The Johnsons were only a few miles from the so-called "red zone." Marcus and I had ridden our bikes to each other's houses dozens of times.

That's it! I realized. Marcus had a bike, and he and I were about the same size. I could use that. I would wake up early in the morning—earlier than anybody would think to wake up on a Sunday—and bike home.

If we wanted our things, I would have to be the one to get them.

I crept out of bed early. Between worrying about Nana and trying to decide on everything I needed to get from the house, I felt like I had barely slept.

Without waking Lupe in the bedroom we now shared, I opened the door and snuck down to the garage where Marcus's bike was kept. I had an empty backpack on my back, ready to be filled with everybody's most precious things—photos, books, shoes, Lupe's camera.

It was about five miles to our house. I figured it would take me about thirty minutes to bike there. I would pack things quickly—in ten minutes or so— and be back to the Johnsons before nine.

Everyone will be so surprised when I return! I thought.

I felt like the only person in the world as I biked through my neighborhood. It was so quiet. The sky was a beautiful blue, and Mount St. Helens looked still and serene, like always, although I could see some steam escaping.

It could have been any other Sunday morning . . . except for the fact that all the cars were missing from the driveways, and there were no dogs barking.

Soon I was coasting the bicycle onto the driveway of the house I hadn't seen in three long weeks. I fished the spare key out of the flowerpot next to our *BIENVENIDOS* doormat and unlocked the door.

"Helloooooooo," I called into the darkness of the living room as the door swung open. "I'm hooooooooooome!"

Of course, there was nobody there to reply.

Leaving the bike on its side by the front door, I made a run for the upstairs bedrooms, taking the stairs two at a time. I went to Mami and Dad's room first, picking up the small stack of library books Mami kept next to their laundry hamper and a pair of Dad's shoes.

In Nana's room, I gently stacked the many picture frames by the bed and slid them into my backpack, adjusting the books and shoes so everything would fit. I tossed the strap over one shoulder.

Just then I heard a buzzing sound, followed by a chirp. It was coming from the living room. It took me a second to realize what it was—Mami's annoying clock, the one that chimed with a different bird sound on every hour and half hour.

It must already be eight-thirty, I realized. The bird chirped on the half hour and sang on the hour.

I better not dawdle, I thought. I wanted to be back before anyone noticed I was gone. Then, when everyone came downstairs for breakfast, I would be there with a backpack full of stuff, like Santa Claus.

Now for Lupe's room. Her camera was there on her bed, right where she had forgotten it the night we left. Thankfully it was packed into its own bag, so I didn't have to cram it into my backpack.

I swung the camera bag onto my other shoulder. *Oof.* It was heavy. As the bed jostled, something small fell off the comforter and onto the floor.

I bent down. It was an inhaler.

Lupe forgot her inhaler?! I thought.

I couldn't believe she had gone three weeks without it, and nobody had noticed. Mami and Dad were forever telling her to keep better track of it.

Maybe this is a spare, and she did *bring one with her?* I racked my brain, trying to remember if I had seen her use one recently.

And then, just like that day at school, the earth moved beneath me. The stable surface on which I stood shook, and I fell down.

I gasped as the wind was knocked out of my chest. Everything in the house rattled. Furniture shook and slid across the floor.

Unlike the earthquake at school, this one went on and on. My teeth rattled. My bones shook. I felt like it would never end.

And then, finally, it was still. I breathed out and slowly got to my feet.

Somehow, I had a gut feeling it wasn't *just* an earthquake. It had lasted *too* long. Things had shaken *too* much.

I dropped my backpack and Lupe's camera bag and flew down the stairs to the kitchen, which had a view of our backyard and, on a clear day, Mount St. Helens.

But when I looked out the window, the sky had disappeared. All I could see was a cloud that looked like cauliflower looming over everything. It was no longer sunny. Everything was gray.

I ran to a different window, one that usually had a view of the mountain. Through the gray, I saw it with its new bulge. But then, as I watched in horror, the bulge crumbled and fell to the ground.

It was no longer a mountain. This was a volcano. And that meant I was in serious danger.

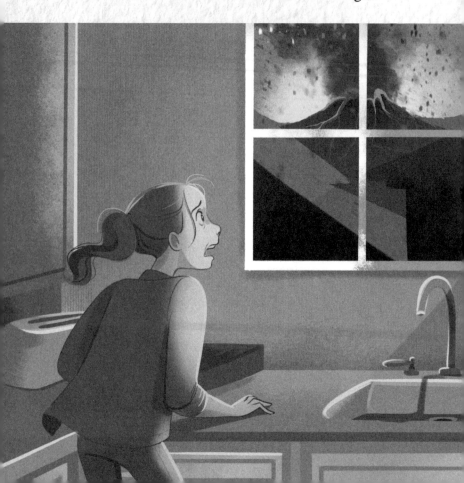

CHAPTER FIVE

Maribel's house
Cougar, Washington
May 18, 1980
8:35 a.m.

My heart was pounding. I reached for the doorknob of the back door and gently pushed it open. As soon as it was open a crack, a gust of hot air smacked me in the face. It felt like I had opened an oven. I quickly slammed the door and jumped back.

What happened? I thought. Just minutes ago, it had been a beautiful day. Now half the mountain was gone.

I didn't know what was coming, how fast the eruption might be heading for me, but I knew one thing for sure: I had to get out of Cougar and back to Yale.

But I couldn't leave without my family's things. Not when I had already come all this way. Not when I knew how much my sister wanted her camera. Not to mention the inhaler I'd found.

I ran up the stairs and back into Lupe's room for my bags. My mind racing as fast as my heart rate, I tried to remember what we had learned at school about disaster preparedness:

Is there going to be lava creeping into my backyard any minute now? Am I going to burn up the second I step outside? How fast can I get out of here?

I was just a kid on a bike. I couldn't drive a car. And even if I could, there weren't any cars here I *could* drive. I wasn't even supposed to *be* here—no one was.

For the past few weeks I had believed what everyone was saying—that people were too worried and *too* prepared. I wanted that to be true so badly right now.

Maybe if I wait a few minutes, the dust will clear, I thought hopefully. *Maybe I can ride back to the Johnsons' like nothing happened at all.*

Somehow I knew that wasn't the case. This was the real deal. Part of the mountain had disappeared into itself. Something was coming this way.

I stuffed the inhaler I'd found in my backpack, put it on my back, and slung Lupe's camera bag crossways across my body. I didn't want it bouncing around as I rode over bumpy streets. Then I raced back downstairs.

At the front door, I stopped. What would I see when I went outside? *Fire?* I thought. *Lava?*

The answer, when I opened the door, was nothing. The air was nothing but dark-gray ash, billowing around as if it were alive. I jumped back and slammed the door shut.

That was it. I wasn't just worried. I was terrified.

I knew I couldn't wait any longer. But even without asthma, I wouldn't be able to ride Marcus's bike if I had to breathe in all that ash.

I glanced around the living room, looking for something to cover my face. My eyes fell on Dad's bandana. I could use that to cover my nose and mouth. I hurried over and grabbed the bandana, but my hands were shaking. It took me three times to tie a good knot.

I made my way back to the front door and took a deep breath—possibly my last one, given all the ash outside. Then I opened the door again and stepped out, slamming it behind me.

Oh no. I stopped. *Where is the house key? Is it in my pocket, or did I leave it inside?*

No time, Maribel! I chided myself. Today was not the day to worry about burglars.

Shielding my eyes with my hands as best I could, I looked around the porch until I glimpsed Marcus's bicycle, lying on its side. It had been bright blue when I left the Johnsons' house. Now it was filthy and gray. I righted it and hopped on, guiding it down to the street.

I began to pedal, resisting the urge to look up at the volcano. I could barely see ahead of me into the street. Not only were there clouds of ash from the eruption, but I was creating little billows myself as I rode the bike. The handkerchief I wore over my face was flapping up and down.

How am I going to know when to turn? I worried. I slowed my legs, pedaling only a few strokes, then coasting, pedaling a few strokes, then coasting again. I didn't want to miss the cross street or run into something in front of me.

You know this neighborhood like the back of your hand, I told myself. If I just calmed down,

stopped thinking about what was happening, maybe muscle memory would take over. Maybe my body would sense when it usually took a left turn.

But it already felt like I had been riding for too long. *Did I miss the turn?*

I focused my eyes downward, looking for things I might recognize: trees or signs or lawn ornaments. I couldn't hear anything but my own heartbeat. No people, no pets, no cars.

I was all alone. It was up to me to save myself.

CHAPTER SIX

Ahead of me, I caught a glimpse of something red. It had to be a stop sign! That meant I was at the end of our street and needed to turn left. I veered toward it to make a left turn.

One street down . . . too many to go.

At least I knew the route to the Johnsons' house by heart. We had driven it so many times before, going back and forth for barbecues, birthday parties, playdates. The ride here, which felt like a lifetime ago, had been so easy—a straight shot most of the way, along Lewis River Road, State Route 503.

Easy, I told myself. But I felt like I was listening to a liar.

I pedaled and pedaled, but it was exhausting. When I rested my legs to coast, the bike went nowhere. I looked down. Part of the front wheel had disappeared underneath dirt, dust, and rocks. It felt like the tire was deflating. The ash from the volcano wasn't just swirling around in the air—it was landing on the ground and burying the street.

Quickly I pushed down on the pedals again before I fell over. It felt like I was riding through quicksand.

I pushed on the pedals, exhaling each time I did so. I tried to gulp more air in, but each time I got a little less. Just a few minutes ago, the handkerchief had flapped in the wind as I rode. Now it was stuck to my nose and mouth, heavy with ash. It was uncomfortable, but I had a feeling if I took it off, it would be even worse.

I pressed down on the pedals one more time, and the bicycle gave up. It wobbled and fell over, taking me with it. I landed in the ash, and a cloud of it blew up around me.

I forced myself to my feet. Dust and ash were in my eyes. I balled my hands into fists and rubbed them. It felt like I was grinding sand into them.

I stared down at the bicycle as fear threatened to overwhelm me. My heart raced. I was just a *kid*.

How did I think I could ride a bicycle through this? Adults could drive cars. Adults could hug me and shield my eyes. I didn't want to be out here.

I would have to walk the rest of the way. It had taken at least thirty minutes to ride *to* my house, and that was with no ash at all.

How long will it take me to walk all the way back? I couldn't have gone more than half a mile before the bicycle gave up. That meant four and a half to go . . . on foot.

I stood with my hands on my hips, trying to catch my breath, and looked back the way I had come. Mount St. Helens seemed to have no shortage of ash, steam, rocks, and dirt to let out. Clouds continually billowed out of what was now a crater instead of a peak.

I could still see the landslide coming my way and felt tears begin to well up in my eyes. I shook my head as if to tell them to stay away.

One foot in front of the other. Think of anything but what's going on around you. Don't look back. I needed to tell myself what to do or I would really start panicking.

I forced myself to start walking. Each step felt more difficult than the last. My sneakers sunk deeper into the ash with every step. Soon I might be buried beneath it.

Isn't there anyone else out here? I thought, looking around. *Someone who went to take a look*

at the mountain? Someone who might have a car?
Someone who might help me?

I coughed and coughed as I walked. The
bandana over my mouth was still there, but it felt
heavy, like it was weighing me down. I lifted up
the flap at my chin to check the air. My lips were
immediately coated with dust.

However uncomfortable the bandana was, it
would be worse without it. I did my best to shake
it out without untying it.

I just wished I was safe in bed at the Johnsons'
house. I wished I had never woken up early. I
wished I hadn't stolen Marcus's bike and left it
behind. I knew he would never see it again . . .
although right now that was the least of my worries.

How long have I been walking? I wondered.
What street am I on?

I looked up, trying to find a building or street
sign to orient me, but even more ash got in my eyes.

I had to shut them. The last thing I had recognized was that stop sign, and that felt like ages ago.

Am I still on the right street? What if I got turned around somehow? I worried. *What if I'm actually walking back where I came from, straight into the mountain?*

I told myself that couldn't possibly be the case. That all I had been doing was walking straight ahead. Even if I wasn't on the right *street,* I was at least going in the right direction.

I needed to do something to keep my mind off my fear of the volcano. The landslide and lava were headed my way, but thinking about that wouldn't make me feel better. I needed to focus on knowing that I would survive.

Survive.

The song!

Everyone at school loved "I Will Survive." We'd all been calling radio stations to request it for the past year. Our teachers and parents were tired of disco and begged us kids to turn it down, but it was so much fun! We couldn't get enough of the music *or* the dancing.

Gloria Gaynor might have been singing about a person, but I was facing a volcano. I wouldn't let it get me.

My voice cracked as I started singing. I knew every word of the song by heart. I coughed over and over again, but I kept singing. It felt like the song was making me walk a little faster.

Just a few more steps and I would be out of harm's way. Just a few more steps and Mount St. Helens wouldn't be able to get me. Just a few more steps and I'd see my family.

"I will survive!"

CHAPTER SEVEN

It felt like I had sung the song a thousand times.
I was hot, tired, and filthy. The air was so thick with
ash that it was impossible to figure out where I was.
For all I knew, I could have been walking straight
into the mouth of the volcano.

Am I the only person left on Earth?

It certainly felt that way. I hadn't seen or heard
from another person since I had left the Johnsons'
house that morning. That now seemed hundreds of
years ago.

Is anyone looking for me? Has anyone even noticed I'm gone? Is it even safe to go back to Yale? How different could things be five miles away?

I imagined everyone was awake by now. I could see them sitting at the dining room table. Mrs. Johnson would be serving pancakes, bacon, and fresh orange juice for breakfast, just as she had every weekend since we moved in. My stomach growled thinking about it. I hadn't thought to eat anything before leaving.

Pass the syrup, Lupe would be saying. She loved drowning her pancakes in them. I preferred just a drizzle of syrup and a lot of butter.

Where's Maribel? someone might be asking.

Oh, probably out for a ride through the neighborhood, Marcus might say. *My bike is missing from the garage. Anyway, what are we doing today for fun?*

I'd thought I was going to bring everyone a great surprise. *I should have left a note,* I berated myself.

I squinted through the ash. It was like stinging hot sand. My eyes hurt too much to open them wider. My ears felt plugged up with ash too.

I had two choices: give up, or keep putting one foot in front of the other.

If I gave up, that meant my trip back home would have been for nothing. And I had to get my sister her inhaler. Even if I was the last person left in Cowlitz County, I would keep walking until I could walk no more.

It felt like I was walking downslope. It may have been the wind that had me disoriented, but I guessed I was near Yale Lake, which meant I was headed in the right direction. The lake was between my house and the Johnsons'.

If I was right, if I could just get my eyes to make out a body of water, I would have a landmark to keep me walking in the right direction. As long as I could keep an eye on the water, I would know that I was walking *away* from the mountain and toward Yale.

I breathed heavily, the bandana fluttering a little less with each exhale as it was covered in more and more ash. I was hot—so hot. I wanted to tear off my ash-covered, hot shirt and pants and throw them as far away from me as I could.

And it felt like it was getting hotter.

Maybe I was wrong about being near water. Maybe I was wrong about what direction I was walking.

But then I heard a faint *whooshing* sound. My heart beat a little faster. I hadn't heard a sound like that this whole time. Was it . . . *water*?

I clenched my fists and took another step. It sounded like the river—a fast, rushing one, like the kind you might go white-water rafting on. But that was faster than our river usually ran.

I took a deep breath, turned around, and immediately froze.

It was *exactly* like the kind of river you might go rafting on. But this wasn't white water. This was dark gray, sloshing around violently, taking bushes and logs and rocks with it.

And it was coming straight at me.

It was rushing faster than I'd ever seen a river go—even faster than in the documentary I'd seen on white-water rafting. I couldn't see very far because of the ash, but as far as I *could* see, there was nothing but a terrible stream of thick, gooey, black ooze picking up everything in its path.

No more walking. I had to *run!*

I turned away from the oncoming flood and took off, running as fast as my legs could take me. Every time my foot left the ground it turned up ash, but I didn't care. I didn't stop, I didn't cough, I didn't think—I just ran for my life.

But I wasn't running fast enough. I could hear the water right behind me. I could *feel* it.

The air was hot all around me. I slowed to a jog—just for a moment—and turned around to look behind me.

All of a sudden, something was burning my arm! I looked down and saw a little spark on the sleeve of my shirt. Before I could even wonder what it was, another spot on my arm sizzled.

This landslide of molten mud, ash, and lava was *burning* me!

I tried not to think about the pain as I began running again, forgetting all about my exhaustion and fear. I didn't want to feel that stinging burn again. I didn't want to be overtaken by this beast.

Every time I looked behind me, I saw the flood of water and debris eating away at the banks, creating a wider black river. I needed to get to higher ground—immediately.

I didn't think I had any speed left in me, but it didn't matter. I had to find some.

I ran and ran, my mouth hanging open. I gasped for breath, my throat raw from inhaling ash, my arm screaming from the droplets that burned my skin.

I ran until I tripped, and then I clawed my way up, grabbing at whatever I could find. It was branches. I had almost run straight into a tree!

I ran again, shooting looks behind me. It wasn't enough to run alongside this thing, I realized. I had to run *away* from it. If I didn't, it would eat away at the ground where I stood and take me along for the ride.

I wouldn't survive that.

CHAPTER **EIGHT**

Somewhere between Cougar and Yale, Washington
May 18, 1980
9:35 a.m.

I adjusted my direction and picked up my
pace again. If I could just get to higher ground,
somewhere more solid than the bank of the river,
which was being eaten away by the lava, I could
slow down. I would be able to start walking again
and make my way to safety.

I stubbed my toe hard into a rock, but I kept
running.

I had a cramp in my side, but I kept running.

My eyes hurt, my arm hurt, my head hurt, but
I kept running.

I was running out of air. I couldn't take in enough breath. I couldn't even feel my legs and feet underneath me.

I was going to fall. I could feel it. I was too tired, too unsteady, too disoriented.

Then, suddenly, something solid—a person!— was right in front of me. I ran into a solid back and bounced right off. For the second time in a day, I was down on the ground instead of standing up.

Oof.

"Oh my goodness. I didn't see you there! Where did you come from?"

It was a woman's voice. I rubbed my eyes with the backs of my hands and shielded them as best I could as I looked up.

I wasn't dreaming. It was a woman, about the same age as Mami. She was covered in ash, as I'm sure I was. She held out her hand, and I grabbed onto it, letting her help me to my feet.

As soon as I was standing, the woman hugged me tightly. Though I didn't know her, I thought it was maybe the best hug I'd ever received in my life.

"What in the world are you doing here?" the woman cried. "Are you alone? What happened? Where are your parents?"

I was so shocked I could barely speak.

"Nancy, quiet down a minute. Let her talk."

That was a man's voice. I could just make him out through the ash as he stepped toward us. He carried a small child in his arms, its hands wrapped around his neck.

"I'm—I mean—I'm—my name is Maribel," I choked out. "Maribel Reyes."

"Maribel, where are your parents?" Nancy asked.

"I don't know," I said slowly. "I mean, I'm alone. I think they're at the hospital with my nana."

"Then how did you get here?" Nancy cried.

"I—I went to get some things. From our house. I was on my way back when the volcano erupted. That's what happened, right? Mount St. Helens erupted?" I asked.

"Yes," Nancy said more calmly. "You should not be out here alone."

I couldn't help myself. I started sobbing. "I know!"

As soon as I said it, everything came pouring out. I began to wail. "I wanted to surprise my sister and my parents with things from home because we were evacuated, so I rode my bike to Cougar this morning. Then the volcano happened and the bike wouldn't move so I had to start walking, and now I don't know where I am!"

Nancy pulled me into her for another hug as I cried. "Shhh, shhh," she said. "It's OK. We found you. We're all together now. You can stay with us."

"I'm so tired," I cried.

"We have to keep moving," the man said. "We're not safe here."

I nodded and coughed. Nancy held out her hand and I took it, grateful not to be alone.

"This is my husband, James," Nancy said. "And that's Elizabeth."

She motioned to the child her husband was carrying . . . a little girl, I realized. She looked to be about four years old, although it was hard to tell given that she was wearing a diving mask. It was smeared with dirt and ash.

All four of us were complete messes. But we were alive.

"How do you know if you're going the right way?" I asked as we resumed walking.

"I don't," James said. "Not for sure. But I have a compass. I can't say I can see it perfectly, but it's what we have."

"I can barely see at all," I said. "My eyes hurt so much."

"That's why I have goggles on!" Elizabeth chimed in.

"Yes," James said. "We're lucky Elizabeth insisted on taking her snorkeling gear on our camping trip. I just wish Nancy and I had brought ours," he joked.

"I'll tell you what," Nancy said, coughing. "That was a smart idea you had covering your face like that, Maribel."

She was referring to Dad's bandana, which I had forgotten I even had on. "I don't think it's helped too much," I croaked.

"Believe me," Nancy said, "it has. You made it all the way here from Cougar, and you can still talk. My throat is raw, and we haven't been out nearly as long as you must have been. We thought staying in the car would be safest, but it didn't take long to realize we would be buried in it if we didn't get out."

I shuddered at the thought. It took me a minute to register what she'd said at first.

"All the way here from Cougar?" I repeated. "Where are we?"

"Well, I can't tell you a precise address," Nancy said, "but we've passed Yale Park, at least. I think we're near the lake."

I hadn't even noticed the park! I must have been running even faster than I'd thought. Or been out here for longer than I'd realized. Would this day ever end?

My parents, Lupe, and the Johnsons had to be looking for me by now. Would they call the police or go out looking for me themselves? Was Yale covered in ash by now? Perhaps they had been evacuated too.

"How far are we going?" I asked.

"As far as we need to go to get to safety,"
James said.

"We need to stay away from the river and try
to stay on high ground," I said, thinking about the
black river I had run away from. I wasn't sure if my
new friends had seen it, but they agreed that moving
somewhere higher up was a good idea.

We walked, stumbling through the ash. We
didn't speak, aside from answering, "We don't
know" each time Elizabeth asked how much longer
it would be.

It felt like the ash was deeper with each step, but
at least there were no longer tiny rocks and hot dirt
raining down on us. That was something.

The trek felt a bit easier now that I had other
people with me. It was a relief to be with grown-ups
and not to feel so alone. I did my best to keep my
eyes peeled for more of the rushing river of molten
goo I had run away from.

I heard a cough and felt a puff of air go by my ear. It was James, who was close behind me. Elizabeth was still on his back.

"OK, Lizzie Bear," he said. "I've got to put you down for a minute. You're getting too heavy for me."

Nancy and I stopped walking and waited as he bent down. Elizabeth slid off his back.

"I'm tired," she whined.

"We all are," Nancy said. "But we have to keep going. You're a big girl. You can walk for a bit. Let your dad rest, and then he'll pick you up again. Here, hold my hand."

"No, I want to hold Maribel's hand," Elizabeth protested.

Before I could say anything, her hand was in mine, gripping me tightly. I wanted to let go, but I kept my mouth shut. She was little, and she was scared.

And to be honest, even though I felt safer now that I wasn't alone, I was still scared too. We didn't know what lay ahead of us or what we might find on the way. We didn't know how long we had to go before we found safety. We didn't even know if there was anyone waiting for us in Yale.

No matter how far we walked, it seemed like we would never escape the clouds and ash of the volcano.

CHAPTER NINE

"Maribel," Elizabeth said, "do you have parents?"

We had fallen into silent trudging again, and I was taken aback by her question.

"Of course I have parents!" I replied—then I had a horrifying thought. Maybe I *didn't* have a family anymore.

Is everyone in Yale safe, or is there ash and lava there too? Are my parents and nana still at the hospital? I thought with increasing panic. *Did they come home in the morning after I left? Can Lupe breathe with all this ash and no inhaler?*

"Elizabeth," Nancy said, gently but firmly, "let's not give Maribel the third degree."

"It's OK," I said hurriedly. "I do have parents. And a nana. And a big sister."

"What's your big sister's name?" Elizabeth asked.

"Lupe," I said. I coughed.

"I wish I had a sister," Elizabeth said. "Mommy and Daddy say maybe next year, but I don't get to pick, so it might be a brother. Boys are gross."

I smiled. Holding her hand made me realize how much I wanted to be with my family.

"I'll tell you what," I said. "Today, I'm your sister."

She squeezed my hand. If I couldn't be with my big sister, I would have to be Elizabeth's. I squeezed her hand right back.

It was getting harder and harder to walk. It was no longer just thick ash and dirt in our way—there were downed trees everywhere we looked. We had to keep looking down so we wouldn't trip on big branches that had been ripped off the trees.

Every now and again, either James or Nancy would scoop Elizabeth up to lift her over a particularly large branch. The second she was on the ground again, she was back to gripping my hand.

It still hurt to keep my eyes open too wide. I doubted I would ever feel like the ash and dirt were out of my eyes. But then, up in the distance, I thought I saw something. I squinted and pointed ahead.

"Look!" I said. "Do you see that?"

Nancy, who was walking in front of me, stopped. She looked where I was pointing. "I do," she said. "What do you think it is? It can't be a house, can it?"

"I don't think we're near any houses," said James.

"Whatever it is, shouldn't we at least check? See if anyone's in there?" Nancy suggested.

"I think we should keep moving," James said. "Who knows what type of building it is or whether it's safe inside."

The adults considered this, silent as we started walking again.

I kept staring at the building, trying to figure out what it was. I desperately wanted to lie down and rest. I imagined it was a beautiful, fancy hotel with plush pillows and blankets on the bed. Maybe it even had a deep bathtub where I could wash all the ash off my body before taking a long nap.

I knew that was impossible. There were no hotels between Cougar and Yale, not even a dirty motel with a creaky bed and thin sheets. But it was nice to imagine.

We were headed straight toward the building, whether we meant to or not. As we approached,

I kept looking around, trying to find some kind of sign to let me know what it was.

Finally, I saw something! Sticking straight up from the ash, as if it had been too proud to fall down, was a sign that read *GAS*.

"It's a gas station!" I cried.

"It couldn't be," Nancy said. "Are you sure?"

"We'd better steer clear," James said.

"What?" I said. "That means we have somewhere to hide. Somewhere to wait for rescue."

"He's right," Nancy said, sharing a look with her husband. "We shouldn't be anywhere near gasoline in a situation like this. It's flammable. Who knows what could set it off."

I frowned. James and Nancy were adults. They must have known what they were talking about. But I was so tired. I knew they were too.

Elizabeth tugged my hand. "Gas station?" she said. "We can get snacks!"

Snacks! my mind screamed.

I knew that was a silly thing to worry about in all this danger, but as soon as she said it, I felt hungrier than I ever had before. I forgot where I was and thought of nothing but all the foods I loved to eat:

A cheeseburger. A sandwich. Nana's tamales. Pan dulces. A milkshake.

I was so hungry, I would even be willing to eat a hundred pounds of spinach!

Focus, Maribel. Focus! Now was not the time to daydream.

"No snacks," Nancy said, shaking her head. "We've got to move on."

"But I'm thirsty," Elizabeth whined.

"We all are," James said. "We're just going to have to wait."

"James," Nancy said quietly, "maybe we should see if there's some water inside. You know, just take a bottle or two with us. You could stay here with the kids while I check it out for safety."

"No," James said. "You stay here. I should check."

"*I* could check," I volunteered. Why should a family be separated? *I* was the one who had joined *them*.

"No way," Nancy said. "We can't let you do that. It's too risky."

"I'll go," James said.

"I will," Nancy insisted.

I didn't like seeing adults so unsure of things. They were supposed to know what to do—always. Maybe I needed to act like an adult now.

"We're going," I said. "All of us. Right now. The quicker we get in, the quicker we can get out and get out of the way."

Before they could say another word, I turned and walked toward the *GAS* sign. Would they follow?

"Wait, Maribel," James called. "We're coming with you."

We all approached the building with caution. I reached for the door handle and pulled. It wouldn't budge. Against the door was a huge mound of dirt and ash.

"We have to get this out of the way," I said.

The three of us bent down and began digging through the dirt with our hands, tossing it out of the way as quickly as possible. Finally, we were able to open the door just enough to slip through. Inside it was dark and quiet.

"Stay here at the door," James said. "I'll go look for water."

"Be careful," Nancy said. She hugged Elizabeth close to her.

James crept off into the darkness. We heard items on shelves rattling when he bumped into them.

"James! Are you OK?" Nancy called.

"I'm fine," he called back. "I think I found some water."

"Hurry back."

When he made it back to us, Nancy and I both breathed out identical sighs of relief. I felt like I had been holding my breath forever.

"I just grabbed the first two bottles I could find," James said. He opened one and handed it to Nancy, who immediately passed it on to Elizabeth. The second one was handed to me.

I gulped it down greedily and almost drank the whole thing. Then I remembered my manners. "Thank you," I said.

"You're welcome," James replied.

I wanted to drink the whole bottle, but I handed it back to share. Nancy and Elizabeth were sharing the other one. We finished them quickly, then stared at each other in the dim light.

"I feel like we should leave some money or something," Nancy said.

"I don't think we should worry about that right now," James said. "We should keep going. I have no idea where this gas station is or how far we've gone."

He pulled his compass from his pocket and tried to wipe it clean with his shirt. It didn't do much. His shirt was filthy.

We shoved the door open again and stepped back outside. After the quick break inside, it almost felt better outside—airier, at least. But a few moments of that and I felt hot and dirty again. The water had tasted so good, but now my throat was raw again.

We made our way back to the road—or what I hoped was the road—and made small talk, trying to pass the time. Nancy and James asked me about school, told me about how much they loved camping, and tried to reassure me that my family was just fine.

"Shhh!" Elizabeth said to us.

"Lizzie," Nancy said, "that's rude!"

"Shhh!" she said again. "Do you hear that?"

We fell silent. At first there was nothing, and then I heard it . . . a low buzzing.

"I hear it," I whispered.

"Me too," said James. He and Nancy looked at each other, then at me. All at once we realized what it was. . . .

"Helicopter!" I cried.

CHAPTER **TEN**

James began waving wildly, looking up in the sky, trying to find it.

"We need to find something to signal that we're here," Nancy said.

I tore off my bandana and began waving it in the air. I stomped my feet in the ash.

"Maribel, what are you doing?" James asked.

"Making a dust cloud," I said. "If we make one that's big enough, maybe they'll see us."

Nancy and James began waving their arms and stomping their feet. Elizabeth jumped up and down.

"Here!" we yelled over and over again. "Down here!"

Our voices were hoarse from all the ash. Could the helicopter possibly hear us all the way down here?

We yelled and yelled, and suddenly, there it was. Our rescue.

Woodland, Oregon
May 18, 1980
1:30 p.m.

"This will be a story to tell your grandkids," the man at the rescue tent said. I had just finished giving him my name and telling him the names of my parents, sister, nana, and the Johnsons.

"But first, let's get you checked out," a woman in a doctor's coat said. "You've inhaled a lot of ash. You'll have to be monitored very closely."

That was fine with me. I had been given water. There were cots everywhere. Finally, I was safe.

Nancy, James, and Elizabeth were already sitting on some cots of their own. I rejoined them when the doctor finished examining them.

"I'm sure your family is worried sick about you," said James. "Hopefully they're somewhere around here as well."

As if he had made it happen, I heard my name being screamed across the room. A second later, I was embraced in a hug.

Lupe! I realized. I wrapped my arms around her, squeezing her tightly. I felt her gasp.

My parents were right behind her, with the Johnsons close behind them. Mami and Dad were both in tears.

"Maribel, we were so worried. How could you leave like that? We didn't know where you were," Mami cried.

The seal burst, and tears poured out of my eyes. "I'm sorry," I wailed. "I went home. I wanted to get our things. I knew we wouldn't be able to go home when you had to take Nana to the hospital."

"We woke up and saw that Marcus's bicycle was missing," Lupe said. "I kept hoping that maybe you had just gone to the park or out on a ride through the neighborhood. But then you didn't come back. I knew you'd gone to the house." She had tears streaming down her face.

"Maribel, *nothing* in our house is as important as you are," Mami said. "That was a very dangerous thing to do. I am so glad you're all right."

"What's this?" Lupe said, reaching around my back.

"What's what?" I asked.

"What are you carrying?" she asked.

The bags! I realized. The day had been so crazy that I hadn't even realized I'd been carrying them this whole time.

"Well . . . ," I said. "I brought you something." I pulled the straps over my head and handed the bags to my parents and sister.

"My camera!" Lupe cried. She immediately unzipped the bag and pulled it out, looking it over like she was worried I might have broken it.

"She brought your inhaler too," Mami said, holding it up in shock. "Maribel, that was an irresponsible decision you made to go home. But it was considerate of you too."

"But never do it again," Dad said sternly. Still, he had a smile on his face. "Family is more important than things."

Family. *After today, I never wanted to be without mine again.* Our house and our things were important, but just being together mattered more. I couldn't wait to see Nana. I even missed the Johnsons. They were almost like family.

"Speaking of family," I said, "this is the family I found. My volcano family." I introduced my parents and sister to Nancy, James, and Elizabeth.

"Thank you for taking care of my Maribel," Mami said to them.

"She took care of us too," James said. "You have a very special daughter."

"We should take a picture of you," Lupe said. She already had her camera out and the strap around her neck. "You won't want to forget any of this—not even how terrible you look."

"Lupe!" Mami scolded.

Nancy laughed. "I'm sure it's true." She put her arm around me. "Believe me, I will never forget this."

James and Elizabeth crowded in with us. Lupe fumbled around with the lens.

"I'm not sure if it's in focus," she said. "It's so dirty I can barely see." She brought it up to her eye.

"Take it anyway," James said.

"Say, 'Volcano,'" Lupe said.

"Volcano!" the four of us cried. The camera shutter snapped.

After taking the photo, Mami wrote down Nancy and James's contact information, promising to send them a copy of the photo and to stay in touch. Then my parents and Lupe took me to the hospital, first to see Nana and then for me to stay the night so doctors could monitor me.

"After all the ash and smoke you've inhaled, it's important to watch your breathing carefully," a doctor said.

Lupe smirked at that. For once, it was me with the bad lungs.

Mami stayed in my hospital room overnight, snoring in a chair next to my bed. But tired as I

was, I couldn't sleep. I looked out the window, where I could just barely see Mount St. Helens in the distance.

I wanted to be sure the mountain was there—that what had happened today wasn't a dream. That my rescue hadn't been a dream, either. But deep down I knew it wasn't. I had survived a volcano. I had gotten myself out of harm's way and back to my family. I hadn't daydreamed. I hadn't given up,

What would Mr. Jennings say about my ability to focus now?

A NOTE FROM THE AUTHOR

The summer before writing this book, I visited Pompeii, located in southern Italy. As you may have learned in school, the town was destroyed by the eruption of the nearby volcano Mount Vesuvius in AD 79.

It's scary to think how something so destructive can also leave things frozen in time. The town of Pompeii and its buildings are so perfectly preserved that it's almost as if everyone simply vanished one day. But the truth is, about two thousand Pompeiians—and about sixteen thousand people overall—died when Mount Vesuvius erupted.

It happened so long ago that it's easy to imagine volcano eruptions are a thing of the past. But the eruption that Maribel survives in this book was very real and quite recent, occurring just a few years before I was born. You may be surprised at how many people in your community might remember seeing the 1980 eruption of Mount St. Helens on the news—or maybe even know someone who lived in the area. Ash from the eruption spread across eleven U.S. states!

For this story, I consulted many maps, videos, and photographs that recorded and re-created the eruption. I crafted Maribel's journey based on that research and those documents. Any errors in geography or topography are my own.

I chose not to let Maribel encounter any dead bodies during her journey to safety, but in truth, approximately 57 people died in the eruption. Part of the reason there were so many deaths is because many people, like Maribel's parents, did not believe an eruption would occur. Mount St. Helens had been burbling and steaming for so many days that it was assumed that an eruption wouldn't be much different. But as Maribel finds out, there is a huge difference between that and an actual eruption.

In cartoons and books, volcanic eruptions and lava are often portrayed as bright red, but in reality, what you are more likely to see is a lahar—a combination of lava, dirt, snow, and ash that becomes a landslide and is more black in color. You can find videos online of these rushing black rivers in action.

Ash and smoke billow above Mount St. Helens following its erruption in Washington state on May 18, 1980.

Near the beginning of the story, Maribel and Lupe learn from one of their teachers that Mount St. Helens is also called Lawetlat-la, or "the Smoker." It was very important to me that I include this information, because what we now call Washington had a name and significance long before European colonists and their descendants came to live there.

The area in which Maribel and her family live is the ancestral and current home of the Cowlitz Indian Tribe and Yakama Nation, among other groups. Lawetlat'la is part of their heritage and home. It's important to honor that and the fact that the United States is a country of occupied land.

Though it is unlikely that she would have been diagnosed in 1980, Maribel exhibits many signs of attention-deficit disorder, or ADD. You may have heard of this condition. It is often misrepresented or exaggerated, showing people who are unable to hold a conversation or sit still in a chair, or depicting them as people who choose not to pay attention.

In fact, ADD is a real medical condition and has nothing to do with choosing to daydream or not caring. For many people, especially girls, ADD is characterized by difficulty focusing or managing time. It's not that people don't *want* to do something; it's that they can't stay committed to one task when their minds are also thinking of many other ideas, tasks, or concepts.

ADD is difficult to deal with, especially when others don't understand what it's really like. There are medications and behavioral therapies that can help people with the disorder be more successful in school, sports, the arts, jobs, and anything else they want to take on! I wanted to make sure Maribel's personal experience with ADD didn't seem like a stereotype.

I had a great time getting to know Maribel, and I'm so proud that she was able to focus her thoughts and be brave, not just for her own sake, but to help her volcano family and "little sister," Elizabeth. The courage, bravery, and determination she showed saved her life. I hope you are never near a volcano when it erupts, but I do hope you have many chances in your life to exhibit your own bravery, just like Maribel!

MAKING CONNECTIONS

1. When Maribel sneaks home, she does so to get belongings that her family loves and values. What are some items your family possesses that would be difficult to replace in a disaster? Why are they important? What do they mean to you?

2. People, including Maribel and her family, found it hard to believe the scientists were right about Mount St. Helens being ready to erupt. That was partly because they were so familiar with the mountain, which was a part of their community and lives. Are you familiar with potential dangers in your community? How are you preparing for them?

3. Maribel has trouble concentrating or staying on task in school, but when the mountain erupts, it is essential that she stay focused in order to survive. Have there been moments in your life where you found it difficult to pay attention? What strategies do you use to stay on track?

4. Ms. Ybarra teaches Maribel and Lupe the name of Mount St. Helens before English-speaking settlers came to the Washington area. There are lands all over America that originally belonged to native and indigenous peoples. Do some research in your community. Who were the original inhabitants? Are they still there, or were they forcibly relocated? What locations do you visit regularly that are significant to indigenous people?

GLOSSARY

ancestral (an-SES-truhl)—coming from an ancestor

ancient (AYN-shunt)—from a long time ago

asthma (AZ-muh)—a condition that causes a person to wheeze and have difficulty breathing

collage (kuh-LAHZH)—a variety of pictures or words cut out from magazines and glued onto a separate piece of paper

considerate (kuhn-SID-er-it)—thoughtful of the needs and feelings of other people

culprit (KUHL-prit)—a person accused of, charged with, or guilty of a crime or fault

dawdle (DAWD-l)—to move slowly and without purpose

disaster preparedness (di-ZAS-tuhr pri-PAIR-id-nis)—steps taken to prepare for and reduce the effects of a disaster

eruption (i-RHUP-shuhn)—the action of throwing out rock, hot ash, and lava from a volcano with great force

evacuate (i-VA-kyuh-wayt)—to leave a dangerous place to go somewhere safer

exasperation (ig-zas-puh-REY-shuhn)—extreme annoyance

geologists (jee-AHL-uh-jists)—people who study minerals, rocks, and soil

hoarse (HOHRS)—having a harsh-sounding voice

inhaler (in-HEY-ler)—a device used for breathing medicine into the lungs

mandatory (MAN-duh-tawr-ee)—required by someone in authority or a government

orient (AWR-ee-uhnt)—to make familiar with a situation or environment

plush (pluhsh)—made of a thick, soft fabric

precise (pri-SISSE)—very accurate or exact

reservation (rez-er-VAY-shuhn)—an area of land set aside by the U.S. government for American Indians

ABOUT THE AUTHOR

Sarah Hannah Gómez has a master's of art degree in children's literature and master's of science in library science. She is now a writer and fitness instructor in Tucson, Arizona. She is working toward a doctoral degree in children's literature at the University of Arizona. Find her online at shgmclicious.com.